The Fourth 100

A COLLECTION OF ONE HUNDRED WORD STORIES

ERICA L. DRAYTON

Copyright © 2024 by Erica L. Drayton

All rights reserved.

No part of this publication may be reproduced, distributed, or transmitted in any form or by any means, including photocopying, recording, or other electronic or mechanical methods, without the prior written permission of the publisher, except as permitted by U.S. copyright law. For permission requests, contact Erica L. Drayton.

All the stories, names, characters, and incidents portrayed in this production are fictitious. No identification with actual persons (living or deceased), places, buildings, and products is intended or should be inferred.

ISBN: 978-1-7339259-4-5

Book Cover by Erica L. Drayton.

First edition 2024.

The Fourth 100

dedication

To my horror and mystery heroes, past and present, who helped me realize my favorite genre to write. Feels like home.

introduction

If you ever questioned my devotion (and some might say obsessive compulsive desire) to write 100 word stories, know that almost every page, including the copyright, introduction, acknowledgments, and blurb on the back are each 100 words exactly.

I can't tell you how or why the bug bit me to give so much of my daily life to the habit of writing in bursts of 100 words at a time but these days I just can't help myself.

This is the first, but certainly not the last, of a series of books collecting my journey with writing 100 word stories.

"The purpose of a storyteller is not to tell you how to think, but to give you questions to think upon."

— Brandon Sanderson

The Fourth
100

Fae

#301

The pain was unbearable but necessary if she was to join her family at the Festival of Lights. She had to go it alone. As much as her mother wanted to be there, hold her hand, wipe her brow, she kept her distance. They all kept their distance.

When the screams started it was visceral. Her skin tore. Two parallel slits on her back. After her screams subsided, the sobs began. She would need to survive the release of her wings. Wet with blood, they unfurled and spread. Each flap felt new but familiar. She was read. She was reborn.

Imp

#302

Sitting at a desk in his study was a rather small man. From behind he was rather nondescript. He wore his favorite bowler hat, and gloves with the finger tips exposed. The room was dark, except for one candle that he used to light the notebook he scribbled in.

Hunched, his waistcoat frayed at the elbows, his bare feet dangled, barely touching the floor. He let them swing aimlessly as he took comfort in the sound of the quill pen scratching the paper.

He spent years working on his memoirs and finally he had the perfect title: The Murderous Imp

Owl

#303

The funeral procession continued well into the night. It was his wishes. To allow his best friends, his only friends, the owls, say their last goodbye. He spent his nights in the woods behind his home, talking to the owls who listened up in the trees.

Little did his family know what he told the owls to do if he died.

As they pushed his casket, on wheels, through the woods, the rhythmic hooting echoed around them. One flew down and landed on the casket. Then another. And another. Till there were dozens. Their heads turned to the future victims.

Mummy

#304

"If I may draw your attention to your left. Here you see Madame Tannarive. In her will she left detailed instruction that her body should be mummified."

The small tour group gasped when they saw a middle-aged woman, so lifelike, sitting at a round table, prepared with tea and biscuits, encased in a glass box. Her hands folded on her lap as if waiting to be served.

"She is having her afternoon tea. And now let us move on to the next room…"

A woman stayed behind, admiring Madame Tannarive's pearl necklace, till she stood up and approached the glass.

Swarm of Light

#305

They wasted little time moving through the abandoned city. No lights were working. What was once a bustling metropolis was now devoid of life. When the swarm of lights first appeared from the sky no one thought they were bad.

But after years and millions of lives lost later, humanity learned very quickly that no one was safe from the lights. Now they hide underground, where no light can penetrate.

Every night four are chosen to breach the surface for supplies and to find anyone stuck, trying to stay out of sight. With time against them, the lights came down.

The Hole

#306

The hole opened up just like that. There was little time to react or consider the consequences of its appearance. We had to jump in and ask questions later.

I took hold of her hand, we smiled at each other, closed our eyes, and jumped. We had no idea how far the fall would be before we reached the bottom. Was there a bottom? And would we die on impact. But the answers were down there. They had to be. We had no other choice.

After what felt like forever we felt a burst of air that helped us land.

The Cheater

#307

"I'm not sure when it started, exactly."

Shirley sucked her teeth. "Yeah, right. The day you don't know when something started is the day we're all out of the game. You just don't wanna own up to what you've been up to."

The other ladies sitting at the booth nodded amongst themselves. They agreed this couldn't go on any longer.

"You never liked me, Shirley. Admit it. That's why you called this meeting. You're jealous that I'm better at this game than you ever were."

"You're a cheater and you know it. You've been cheating ever since you joined us."

The Waves

#308

The waves brought her home. After weeks of drifting with the tide she thought her life would end in the middle of the ocean.

Then her small boat, with no oars or sail, washed up onto land. She woke from a sleep where food was plentiful and drink never stopped flowing. Her mouth was dry and stomach empty. She would do anything for a taste of her dreams.

She spilled out over the boat and let the water wash over her, awakening her senses. Her nose led to food found inside shelter that didn't belong to her, but does now.

The Book

#309

Some books should never be opened. Especially, the ones that contain secrets. They can open a door to a new world or trap you inside another.

When she saw the book, once locked away, opened to a random page, she knew her life was in danger. She looked over at the chapter it fell open on: It Walks at Night.

She didn't need to read any further to know the kind of trouble she was in. With little time to lose she started to retrace her step back outside. But before she could reach the exit a growl stopped her.

The Spotlight

#310

Did Matilda somehow orchestrate this? She was not a woman of significance so no one guessed she was behind it all. The party was going so well. We all were dancing and singing and drinking, unaware of our fates.

But all that was about to change when the lights went out. The music stopped. Wine glasses shattered hitting the floor.

"Ladies and gentlemen, we are sorry for the inconvenience. It's time for a different kind of party to begin. My kind of party."

A spotlight came on. The first person it landed on disappeared. Then moved on to the next…

The Kill Shot

#311

It tasted like lightning. And although I knew I must be dead I wasn't ready to go. I wasn't going out like this. It was just one bullet in the chest and blood instantly spewed from my mouth. I spat one time. The burn from the bullet created wisps of smoke as I walked towards the gunman.

I don't think he was prepared for me to lunge at him. Who would be after just delivering a kill shot. But I found myself feeling surprisingly powerful, not to mention, really fucking pissed.

I grabbed his gun and turned it on him.

The Mirror

#312

He looked at his reflection; there was something about it. He never liked to look at himself in the mirror, afraid of what he might see, or not see. Until, one day he received a package with no return label. He wasn't expecting a mirror and found himself staring at it for what seemed like hours before putting it away.

The next morning, he peeked and didn't recognize himself. As long as he never looked in a mirror he could imagine whatever he wanted to look like.

Now, faced with the truth, he didn't like the monster in the mirror.

The Judge

#313

"Today's the day," she whispered. The courtroom was buzzing with spectators sitting in the gallery and the judge behind the bench. Taylor found a seat near the back and took it right as things were getting started.

"Order. Order," the judge said, banging his gavel. He scanned the room and locked eyes with Taylor in the back. From the moment he saw her his demeanor changed for the rest of the day.

The last case done for the day, Taylor walked through the crowd. No one saw her. She approached the bench. The judge also knew, today was the day.

La Fea

#314

He had always preferred daggers. They were lightweight and easier to conceal. Which is why he wasn't too concerned when he found himself surrounded by a group of thugs one night. He knew there was a bounty on his head.

No one stole from La Fea and got away with it.

He seemed unarmed as they circled him, brandishing their weapons in the hopes of intimidating him. Maybe he'll give back what he took as a bargaining chip for his life?

Instead, he laughed out loud. "Me río porque La Fea mandó a todos aquí a morir. Isn't that funny?"

The Target

#315

He knew he wasn't coming back from that assignment. But that was what he wanted. He had been in the game for a long time and wanted to go out on top. When he got the call and was sent instructions on his target he knew this was the one.

He had a plan and even though he knew the outcome, he was ready. First, he learned his targets movements. Where it would be at all times and when it would be alone.

After months of surveillance he made his move even when he heard one bullet enter the chamber.

The Picnic

#316

John and Lucy went to the riverside. John packed their lunch. All of Lucy's favorites. Roast beef sandwiches, potato salad, and a dozen fresh donuts. The entire drive to the riverside they talked about the good old days. The happiest times they spent together.

Lucy packed the blankets because John always forgot the blankets. With a special gift hidden inside like she always did whenever they made time to get away from their busy lives.

They found their favorite spot by the river where a large tree provided shade. John carried the basket and Lucy brought the blanket and gun.

The Tree

#317

The rain tore through fresh blossoms on the ancient tree. As if commanded, it started and washed away all the evidence of anything having happened. A life ended. Blossoms falling with the wind till they landed on the cold, wet ground.

Footprints in the soft earth now turned to mud and puddles pooling around the base of the ancient tree. Planted centuries ago it was time to feed again. Its roots pushed up to the surface and wrapped around the once vibrant soul that now lay lifeless.

Slowly they pulled the body down, beneath the surface, to feed the tree.

The Payout

#318

I wanted so badly to ask for help. I sat in my car and waited like the note said to do. I had a problem that required someone with a better track record than my own to deal with it. All I had to do was sit and wait.

My passenger door opened and he sat down next to me. "Do you have the money?"

I handed him a fat envelope of money that he took, no questions, and left my car. I asked for help and now there was no turning back.

I gripped my steering wheel and screamed.

The One

#319

I thought you were the one for me. And you warned me what might happen if I stayed, but I stayed anyway. Even after they dug up your backyard. After you went on the run from the police.

I know you're out there somewhere. I know you'll come back for me.

They think I was your partner in crime. They think I have it in me to do what you did. Will they ever uncover just how right they are? Only if they decide to dig up my backyard.

Do you think they'll be surprised when they find you there?

The Flower Show

#320

To everyone's surprise, Charles never arrived at the flower show. The judges started their walk through of each display. Clipboards in hand they made their arbitrary marks.

The closer the judges got to Charles' display the more the whispers became about where he could be. He was never one to miss this part of the competition. His floral display had won top prize three seasons in a row and everyone knew this would be his year again.

When the judges flanked his display one gasped, another turned away and the third fainted. The spectators tried to get a closer look.

The Operation
#321

When she woke up, the pain was excruciating. They told her there would be a little discomfort. The thought of getting out of bed terrified her. Then she felt a distinct chill down her spine.

Her eyes darted around the room, trying to speak but words just wouldn't come. She managed to move her left hand over and found the bed controls to raise her head. A mirror opposite her bed showed her something she was not prepared to face. A tear rolled down her cheek.

"Ladies and gentlemen, Subject 31624. Show of hands, who's in?"

Everyone's hands went up.

The Farm

#322

I was like you once, then everything changed! I bought a farm from an ad in a paper. I thought it was a joke at first. The description just seemed too good to be true. There must be a catch, but I needed out of the city.

When I arrived at the farm I was greeted by an agent at the gate who informed me I must make an offer sight unseen. My first tip-off that something wasn't right. But from my vantage point it looked incredible.

He couldn't hand me the keys fast enough. This farm would be trouble.

Spotlight

#323

"In this room we keep her most prized possessions…"

The tour guide's voice faded away when I saw it. I couldn't believe I was a few feet away from her wand. The stories I'd heard about it up until this point are epic.

It rested on a fluffy red velvet pillow on a pillar with one spotlight pointed directly at it. In the room were other things that belonged to her but none had quite the same level of importance for me. I had to have it—

"Stay together please!" I rejoined the tour, leaving the spotlight pointing at nothing.

Two Paths

#324

"Are you sure about this?" We stared at the fork in the road, an unfinished map between us. Torn just before the X that marks the spot.

We could go left, where the path seemed clean and clear. Trees tall and thriving, letting through the light of a setting sun. Or we could go right, where the path wasn't so clean or clear. I turned on a flashlight just to see what was up ahead. Fallen limbs and vines left us wondering what creatures we might encounter.

"Do we want safety," I asked, pointing left, "or mysterious adventure," pointing right.

Company

#325

Taking the right path was wrong. We realized that after walking for about an hour through the dense forest, expecting to find what we were looking for before whatever lived in here found us first.

"This is pointless. Let's turn back," she said, and sat down on what looked like a stump.

"Tsk. Tsk. Tsk." The voice was sharp and shrill, echoing through the trees.
"Who said that? Who's there?" I asked.

"We wouldn't turn back if we were you. The road less traveled is a better plan for two."

Along the path, two pair of red eyes watched us.

Wen and Fen

#326

Out of the darkness they pranced, holding hands and humming a song I couldn't quite understand.

"What are they supposed to be?" She asked. All I could do was shrug and watch them dance around us.

"We are Wen and Fen. Who are you?" They said, though I can't confirm I saw their mouths move. I wasn't sure they had mouths. And though their limbs numbered four, I couldn't say they were human or animal.

"Listen, we mean you no harm. We're just looking for—"

They giggled loudly then said in unison, "The more you look, the less you'll find."

Rat Game

#327

I never wanted to follow Wen and Fen. There was something about them that I didn't trust. But they said they could help us find what we were looking for. We had to believe them.

So, they took us to meet their mother, a woman who had all the answers we needed.

"Do you play?" She pointed to a tree that had a dead rat nailed to it. Then she picked up an axe and sent it sailing through the air, eventually cutting the rat in half. "If you can do better I'll tell you what you want to know."

A Win & A Lie

#328

The axe was light in my hand and I threw it like I'd played this game many times before. They certainly all looked at me like I had. Then I was victorious and the win, bittersweet. But we still had a long journey ahead of us. I was certain of that.

Begrudgingly, she gave us the answer to the rest of our map. Taking what was once torn and lost and breathing new life into it. Our story would continue. This would not be our end.

Would that I wasn't such a trusting person, I might have spotted the lie!

Red River

#329

It wasn't long after we departed that we realized we weren't in Swindle anymore. A town no one could ever find on a map and now we knew why. Who would want to? No one. Maybe it was the bridge we crossed or the river that ran under it, more red than blue or green.

"Tell me again why we can't turn back now?" It was a question she managed to ask so many times my answer each time was shorter and shorter.

"Because," I said, and pressed on across the bridge.

"I'm afraid this is where your journey ends."

Mosquito

#330

If I'm being honest, he was a rather polite mosquito, even if he does have an uncontrollable hunger for blood. Standing at the other end of the bridge in a three piece suit, red suede shoes, and bowler hat with a bright red rose in his lapel, he politely asked us to follow him.

She gripped my hand tighter when we saw the train. With little options but to get on, we found ourselves moving on a track we didn't even know existed till now.

"I must say, the pair o' ya are much more trusting than the last two."

In Case of Emergency

#331

Trapped on a train with no idea of its destination. A rather large mosquito for company. And an unfinished map leading to a promise of something unlike anything we could ever imagine.

If there was ever a time for me to step up and take control of the situation, it was now. I smiled innocently while I looked around for a means of escape. There was one window with bars on the outside and a door at either end, both blocked by large crates with air holes.

Painted in red, on each, were the words "Break in case of emergency."

Break Free

#332

While the mosquito chattered away, I looked around for something I could use to break one of the crates. I had a feeling whatever was inside would be distracting enough to help us escape.

I jumped up, grabbed the chair I sat on and hurled it at one of the crates. They both shattered on impact to reveal a lizard wearing glasses, reading a book.

He lowered his glasses, stared me straight in the eyes and asked, "Is this a case of emergency situation?" I can't remember what I said. All I knew was I had talked to a lizard!

Don't Trust the Chicken

#333

Suddenly, the train car was thrust into darkness and our new lizard friend was kicking butt. Turns out lizards move faster and fight better than I thought.

"Follow me," the lizard whispered in my ear. I grabbed her hand and together we ran to the next car.

"Do you know where we're headed?"

"Sorry kids, this is where I get off. Thanks for saving my life. They would've sold me for sure if you hadn't set me free. Take my advice, whatever you do, don't trust the chicken." Before I could ask what he meant, he leapt from the train.

Pumpkin Head

#334

It wasn't long before we reached our destination. What was waiting for us on the platform was not what either of us were expecting. Which is saying a lot since we had just been kidnapped by a mosquito and rescued by a lizard.

"Is that a scarecrow with a pumpkin for a head?" She asked me.

"You flatter me, madam. I'm here to escort you to the castle."

"And if we don't want to?" I asked. Though secretly I wanted to.

The pumpkin head smiled. "Now, you don't wanna go around saying something like that. You'll hurt the queen's feelings."

The Caged Bird

#335

Her cage was massive. I have never seen a cage that large before. She ruffled her feathers and turned her head. Her beak poked through the bars.

"Why are you here?" Her question took us by surprise. Not because she was a large and plump chicken, but because she was trapped in a cage.

"You brought us here. We were just passing through."

She cackled. No, clucked. "I can help you but you must tell me the truth."

"What can a caged bird do?"

Suddenly, her cage door opened. It was then I wished I hadn't opened my big mouth.

The Kid

#336

"Bring out the kid," she clucked. We heard the rattling of chains, then a boy with shackles around his wrists and ankles appeared, led by two lizard guards.

"What's the meaning of this? Where did you get him from?"

"Why is it your kind always ask the wrong questions. What you should be wondering is why we felt the need to chain him up. You'll soon find out." She gave the signal for the kid to be released, then returned to the safety of her cage.

The kid looked at us with hunger in his eyes and said, "I'm hungry."

A Blue Suit

#337

The gentleman wore a blue suit,
When he walked into the lake.
With a gun prepared to shoot,
He knew what it would take.

The lake was only waist high,
But there was no place left to run.
Here is where he's meant to die,
In that moment he dropped the gun.

And cried into the lake of tears,
For all the time he wasted.
And the many grueling years,
When he felt hated.

Now he'll get his own back,
And teach them all a valuable lesson.
Of the kindness that they lack,
Before he sends them straight to heaven.

Night Fight

#338

When the men went walking through the night
They gathered all their weapons
All of them prepared to fight

Pitchforks, bats, chains, and knives
Were they all prepared to die?
None of them had told their wives

And when the rain began to fall
The clouds grew black
The spiders gathered on the wall

To watch the battle about the unfold
Between the men and beasts in kind
The former most naive and bold

They raised their weapons in the air
A crack of lightning—broken silence
There was little here to fear

Blood was shed
But who was dead?

The Moving Rock

#339

The rock was nestled in the sand.
Placed there in a time before man.
It was its home for centuries on
Watching life and nearly gone.

With the storm clouds rolling in
Another layer of life comes to an end.
The rock comes loose from the sand,
And moves as if by God's hand.

Lightning sparks the pitch black sky,
Then the heavens start to cry.
The rock continues 'cross the shore,
A last chance for something more.

A rock that once was stuck on land,
Leaves behind its endless plans,
For an uncertain world,
In the waters of old.

A Long March

#340

The funeral march began at dawn
Pallbearers numbered six in all
Stood shoulder to shoulder
A casket between them

No one knew who was inside
A death less important than the journey
Down the streets where all could see
They marched and marched endlessly

Everyone joined in time
The children mimicking their adults
The adults mimicking their ancestors
Of a ritual not long forgotten or fully remembered

Until the sun began to set
And whispered glances watched—waited
For the moment when the casket's opened
Whoever's inside left with a decision

Rise and face the world alone
Or return home

When Mourning Comes

#341

Sunlight shone upon her red hair splayed on the grass
The entire night spent sleeping under the stars
Birds chirping their mourning songs on branches.

Soon her parents will awaken when the cock crows
And tend to their chores as farmers do
Never wondering where their daughter might be this mourn

By afternoon the father wipes his sweaty brow
As he trudges towards the water well for a drink
Footprints in the dirt mask where she had been

Then mother calls out for her daughter
And wonders where that silly dreamer could be
Laying still upon the grass till mourn.

Gwendolyn

#342

He rode upon his trusty steed,
To duel a man about his greed,
For food and wine and women too
It was the noble thing to do.

The helmet upon his head grew hot
But they rode on—he would not stop
When suddenly he felt a pain
His leg warned him of rain.

Lightning struck a tree close by
A limb came crashing from the sky
And landed right in front of the horse
With little time to change their course.

They galloped over the fallen limb
To fight a battle they'll surely win
For the heart of Gwendolyn.

Masquerade

#343

We all wore masks to hide our face
From such a vile and ghastly place.
We chanted and we drank all night
Till morning came with first light.

Some were tired and so they slept
While others knew the outcome and wept.
For the youth gone by so soon,
And the laughter left behind with the moon.

No one wanted to remove their mask,
A common revolt from the simple task.
When morning comes we must reveal,
Our one true selves, that was the deal.

I removed my mask and tossed it away,
Ready at last to seize the day!

Midnight Riders

#344

The midnight riders use the light of the moon
To deliver them on wings of doom,
Across the bridge, through shallow streams,
They will enter your every dreams.

While you slumber in your beds,
The midnight riders sneak into your heads.
Making subtle suggestions about your life,
Leaving sharp cuts like a knife.

Should you wake before they're through,
Take care, for they'll come after you.
And make you pay for crimes of sleep,
All the pain—regrets you'll keep.

But if you can survive by dawn,
The midnight riders are all gone,
Expecting you to live and carry on.

Willow Weeps

#345

She pressed her hand upon the tree
And listened to it carefully.
It spoke of sadness and of war,
It whispered dangers at her door.

The willow weeped for what had been,
And begged her never to come again.
There was no saving this great tree
The time had come to set it free.

The memories of what it had seen
The people who sat upon the green
And made their plans for life—for love
Never noticing the tree above.

It shouted warnings to them all,
Don't pretend—or try to be strong.
That which stands will always fall.

Eileen

#346

He walked into town with a satchel slung over his shoulder,
Looking for the girl he named Eileen.
She wore yellow ribbons upon her red hair.
He was much older now but remembers her well.

In her youth she'd run to try and catch butterflies,
Never understood creatures need to be free.
She grabbed his finger in her little hand,
He walks with her still even when no one else will.

She met him there in the center of town,
Where he said he'd be one day.
Her yellow ribbons faded and butterflies are caged.
She wasn't his girl anymore.

Stop the Beat

#347

When the band began to play everyone got on their feet
Swaying to and fro to the rhythm of the saxophone
Then the piano joined in and the drums followed close behind
Dancing to the sinner man's beat.

It went on and on for nearly an hour
Exhaustion settled in but no one could stop
Even the players started to show signs of madness
Someone else had all the power.

They shouted for the music to stop
Begged and pleaded to relieve their minds
Of the endless chords that played
As the beat continued on—people suddenly began to drop.

Dinner Party

#348

She watched them all from a distance
A host preparing her final speech
To tell her guests about a murder
Happening before the feast.

They all were chosen quite specifically
For the deeds they'd done in life
And the crimes they have committed
None of them would leave alive.

She made her way to the center of the room
And held up a glass prepared to clink
But her action was cut short
By the spilling of a drink.

The distraction caused a stir,
All the guests very much unaware
Of their fates as yet announced
Everyone had better beware.

The Plant

#349

She bought a plant at the corner store and brought it home,
This she did, and nothing more.
She watered the plant so it would grow big and strong,
This she did, and nothing more.

Till one day it bloomed, purple and red and orange too
This it did, and nothing more.
Then they began to move and speak, discussing what to eat,
This it did, and nothing more.

Hungering for human flesh the plant did walk up to her room,
This it did, and nothing more.
But she waited with an axe,
This she did,
and that
was
that.

Conductor

#350

The conductor tapped the orchestra to attention,
raised his arms high and waved the baton back and forth.
This cued the drums, low and slow.
His arms came down with gusto and intention,
the drums grew louder.
Then the violins and strings began to play.

He bobbed his left hand up and down for tempo.
Cueing other instruments with this baton,
his hair disheveled by his staccato head movements.
He pointed the baton at the orchestra and raised them higher,
his hands shook from the power,
the music.

Then he stopped,
put his baton down,
and left the empty stage.

Build a House

#351

They built the house, brick by brick,
Laid the foundation over years of heart break.
Doors to let the good times in,
Windows to shut the evil out.

But the windows shattered over time
And sickness blew in like the setting of a thousand stars
The house needed work but the people inside
Creaked with age and an unfinished frame.

She died before they finished the house,
So hammered and nailed and cried tears
Then he dropped his tools,
Bid the house farewell
After so many years it could no longer hold him
Without her, living inside was a lie.

Jolly Robber

#352

The manner of the jolly robber,
Is quite passive and doesn't bother,
With the jewel around her neck,
He sees better on the deck.

Lords and ladies walk two by two
Board the ship and admire the view
As they prepare to sail away,
For the promise of a brighter day.

On day three the crew rebelled,
Everyone's sick and didn't feel well.
Turns out a disease was brought on board
Biding time then attacked the horde.

No one was safe from the deadly disease
Except the jolly robber who felt at ease,
Till he fell down to one knee.

Not Ugly

#353

The scars upon her face reveal,
A side of her that cannot feel.
It's where she hides away from the world
Just a lonely girl, alone
Trying not to come unfurled.

She sits at the piano and plays
The notes that speak what she can't say
A piece she learned long time ago
When she was loved for what's inside
And her scars began to show

She remembers how she looked before
A beauty to everyone and more
Her smile could brighten any room
But inside she couldn't escape
The scars she always saw on her face

Was she real?

Skinwalkers

#354

Beware the Skinwalkers,
with claws as sharp as nails.
They walk on two legs,
and once they attack they never fail.

There's danger in the woods at night,
so never walk alone.
They'll back you up into a corner,
and rip your skin off to the bone.

Its eyes can see you in the dark,
you mustn't turn your back on them.
Skinwalkers can be anyone,
they can even be your best friend.

But remember you can hurt them too,
if you dare to stand and fight.
Just bring a weapon you can wield,
and you just might survive tonight.

[PERIOD]

#355

Scoop my guts out with a shovel—
curled up in a fetal position,
cry and cry and cry.
Scream into my pillow,
while the pain grows and grows,
and grows.

It's a part of life, to bring life, and be life.
Can't escape it—must embrace it.
Excruciating day and night life.

Solid as a clock—works,
steady as an ungrateful friend.
Turns and churns from deep within,
burns and gurgles, then settles in.
Lasts for days, but never ends?

Aging is my only out!
Older! Older! Older!
Freedom's coming to me soon?
Then I'll sweat and sweat—
Hello womanhood…

Nonsense

#356

I chanced upon a grizzly bear,
it happened whilst I was out last year.
Never had I seen such a beast,
on all fours and ready to feast.

In the distance I also did hear,
the screeching of tires drawing near.
I hopped in the car, but didn't go far,
for we wanted to stop at a bar.

I got pretty drunk,
smelled of booze like a skunk.
Then I started to ramble,
till I found me a great place to gamble.

Now you all may praise me,
for my earlier crime spree,
where all I will say,
is hooray!

Road of Dreams

#357

There is a road where none exists,
and comes with the rising of the moon.
It goes to a place, a far away land,
then disappears with the break of day.

The road quickly vanishes,
but the sounds of the people fails to fade.
They walk amongst us even now.
Listen carefully to their laughter and cries.

Their souls can only live in darkness,
hidden away from our eyes of judgement.
One day they hope to see the sun again.
Be part of us, dance and sing again.

Until that day they hide away,
along the hidden road of dreams.

The Message

#358

Years **Of** sUrrender gone in a whisper
and **Trouble** sHeds **Its** Nightly sKin
because skY gOds are Under clouds
and Kings Need sOme Water to drown
in MEadows where the sycamore grows.

Yet weather's gOne hiding Underground
tHe night mAkes us Victors and hEalers to the needy
but what caN becOme of the small yet
Insignificant man anD his Earlier plAns to die

Try telling your tale to tHE crowds who don't care
who QUestion Every ExterNal move you try to make
And wilL you With A Yearning to See the rising
sWelling tIdes that siNk even the mightieSt ships

Too Soon

#359

The pendulum swung from side to side
It never stopped, it never died.
For it the pendulum stops it's swing,
The whole world must begin again.

In mixed expressions from on high,
Lightning crashed down from the sky.
It split a tree and broke the earth,
Signaling the dawning of a new birth.

Until such time as dawn should rise,
No one would question or even try.
Till danger brought a tree right down,
And forced us all to blame the clown.

With faces full of yesterdays sad news,
Accepting all the verbal cues,
To say goodbye—gone too soon.

On the Line

#360

Terrible and bitter sweet,
She checks on her garden and tends to her clothes—
Hanging on the line,
Blowing in the wind,
Drying under the hot Summer sun of the day.

She thinks no one's watching
As she sways to the music carried on the wind,
A bird perches on the limb of a tree,
Watching her every move—waiting.

Another joins the bird…then another—
Then four more.
She keeps on dancing her tuneless score,
Smiling at a neighbor jogging by.

They look up at the birds
Run faster! Get away!
Soon there'll be another feeding,
A bird buffet.

Pianist

#361

With trembling fingers and beating heart
She sat up straight in her chair
A bead of sweat threatening upon her brow
There was no backing out
Only thing to do was start

The keys she tapped came naturally
Her fingers played each note
Feeling the instruments that joined in
The sheet music a distant memory
She only need listen to her heart

The bead of sweat fell with little notice
Followed by another
Worried that she may never finish
Before her time would be cut short
Then she saw red upon the keys

She cried and touched her last key.

Not Earth

#362

We looked to the sky for their sign
They said keep watch, help was coming
Two decades gone and not a word or signal
Hope dashed away on the tale end of stars

Every night a comet flies by
We are planets away left alone and abandoned
Waiting for hope to eventually come
Have they forgotten us like the setting of the sun

On a mission to find life
Instead we rather end life
None of us wanted this life
Where is our promised new life?

In the dust of a forgotten planet
Look beyond the stars to find us.

Just a Game

#363

It was just a game,
That's what everyone kept telling me
But where were their voices
When the game turned deadly?
And my life was on the line.
Now no one has words
Only empty explanations
They try and try to be more caring
About a choice, a move, a crime.

It wasn't a game.
There were definitely rules.
I broke every one—
Faced with consequences in the mirror.
My choice, my move, my crime.
I tried to be more caring
Talk myself through fake accusations,
Your life on the line
The game has just begun
But I'm walking away.

She

#364

She ran like the wind when no one was chasin'
Not a care in the world when things were easy.
And she jokes with her friends at the end of the day,
They're gone now—in her heart they stay.

She says when she grows up she'll still laugh and smile
But she's changed—she's not the same.
And the friends in her life, they come and they go,
She can't help herself, they need her, she knows.

At the end of her life she'll sit down and say
It was fun, I was happy,
I did it my way.

In the River

#365

The river raged with souls untamed
Of those who never had a name,
They must go where the water takes them
Hoping home will come again.

Take them to an unknown place
Where everyone has a face,
And speaking truth is met with grace
To get there we must stop this chase.

Now the raging river has calmed
To let us through the great beyond,
Please wait for me if you get there first
I'm drowning yet I feel such thirst.

Against the river we all must go
Fear not the dangers of below
It is safer than you know.

My Story

#366

This was harder than I thought,
Everything is harder than I thought—now,
That I am older,
Not wiser.
But I can laugh through it and you can't.

It's not about the stories told,
If not me then someone else—
Will tell my story—better? faster?
Sometimes I feel like a disaster.

I do this not for any glory
You could never tell my story.
I do this for the fame,
Please—don't forget my name…

I've finally found a place familiar
I'm settling in—I am your killer
Remember that it's just a story
And I wield the pen.

The Jump

#367

She waited on the edge of the platform. It was late enough that hardly anyone was around. Just a homeless man muttering to himself on a bench. But if he noticed her, it was irrelevant.

This was her last chance to enter the other world. A place she had never been but read about, and imagined, from the journals of her ancestors.

She felt the rumble of the train before she heard its loud horn. A warning that it would not be stopping. Now or never. Alice looked back at the homeless man. He winked at her before she jumped!

The Watcher

#368

The homeless man stood over her body on the tracks, shook his head and sucked his teeth. He spit out the side of his mouth, pushed up his dirty jacket sleeves and hopped down beside her.

He grabbed under her shoulders, lifted, and dragged her along the tracks till they were both deep within the tunnel. This was his job but he was older now, more out of breath.

He felt for a knob and opened a door to a room where there were three other girls laying on long tables. He placed her on an empty table and left.

It

#369

She was no longer in a train station, on a platform, waiting for a train to come racing down the track. Her eyes opened and she felt the cold ground beneath her. Darkness all around, except for a bobbing light headed straight for her.

She managed to sit up. Her head throbbing. As the light got closer she heard a voice calling out to her, "Where have you been, child. We've been searching everywhere for you. Come along, quickly, before it gets us."

"Wait, how do you know who I am?"

"Never mind that. Did you bring it with you?"

An Old Friend

#370

"I feel like I've been hit by a train."

"That's because you have, dearie, and if you haven't—" the jackalope stopped short when he saw the gold and red scarf around her neck. "Yes! We're saved!"

The girl tried to stand but stumbled. The jackalope stood seven feet tall when on its hind legs and caught her with its front hooves. She looked up at his massive antlers in awe.

"What…are you?" She asked, unafraid. It was as if she knew him.

"My name is Jack. But, there isn't time for reintroductions. The Queen has sent it after us."

The Run Away

#371

Together they walked through the forest in search of a place to hide. "What is it that was sent after me?"

"I'm not really sure. I just know you wouldn't want it to catch you." Jack shook his head back and forth. "Wait! Listen." His ears perked up and he jutted out his antlers.

"What are you doing?" She asked, frustrated with herself that she was in a familiar place but couldn't quite remember how or why.

"I'm listening. You should do the same. I can hear someone approaching." Jack's voice wavered. "This is where I must leave you, dear."

Butterfly

#372

Terrified of what was out there watching her, she stood tall, squared her shoulders and shouted, "who are you?"

A sudden wind kicked up around her, howling in the air. Her long auburn hair blew in her face then stopped. When she moved her hair from her eyes she saw a butterfly standing taller than she, with part of one wing bent and damaged.

"You are the one who has returned. Why?" It flapped its wings when it spoke, nearly knocking her off her feet.

"I can't remember—"

"I can't remember," it echoed. "Follow me. You haven't much time left."

The Maze

#373

She held on to the butterfly's broken wing as they walked together through the darkness. Having never spoke to a butterfly before she was unsure of what to say but she trusted it would not harm her.

"This is where you'll get lost and lose and leave me," the butterfly said, a sense of sadness in its voice. "Why do you always leave?"

"I don't want to leave. Why do I get lost?" she asked but her answer came when the sun began to rise and she was faced with tall hedges in the shape of a most inviting maze.

Multiplicity

#374

The butterfly disintegrated under the scorching sun. Its ashes swept away by a quiet wind that blew through her hair and pushed her towards the entrance of the maze.

The maze was so tall it provided shade from the sun, but also made finding her way very difficult. Symbols on plaques that she could not decipher frustrated her, and she swore there were voices whispering through the hedges. Watching her. Giggling.

"You'll never make it," came a voice from the top of the hedge. She looked up and saw an owl. "There are three of you lost in here already."

Meal

#375

Under cover of darkness walked a proud lion on its hind legs. A scarf wrapped around its neck, and walking stick in its right paw used to stand upright. A pipe hung from his massive mouth and a signet ring shone in the darkness. He eyed the girl passively.

"You're standing in my way. If I were not already quite full from devouring you the other day…" he scoffed before continuing his stride around her.

"Excuse me, Lion. Do you mind if I follow you?"

He smiled down at her. "Certainly. One never knows when the next meal will come."

Drunk

#376

She stayed close to the Lion, but not too close. Suddenly, he swung his cane out to stop her.

"Did you hear that?" The Lion sniffed the air and growled loudly. "Who's there? Show yourself."

The girl hid herself behind him and listened closely. A tiny light bounced and swayed back and forth, then side to side, near the ground. The Mouse managed to stand still long enough for her to see before continuing its drunken march.

The Lion yelped with terror before scampering away on all fours. The Mouse burped an 'allo' and smiled before he passed out, snoring.

Sober!

#377

The little girl knelt over the drunken Mouse, when a Rabbit appeared out of nowhere. So tall it looked over her shoulder and down at the Mouse, shaking its head.

"You will have to excuse my friend. He went at the sherry a bit too hard this evening and these are the consequences. You wouldn't want to try some, would you?" The Rabbit held out a flask to the girl. She'd never had sherry before and was curious what it tasted like.

She took one small sip when suddenly the "drunk" Mouse seemed to jump to its feet. Quite sober.

Big Head

#378

She woke in a strange place. Her head swimming from the drink she sipped.

"Finally," the King said, high upon his throne. The girl looked over at him, unimpressed. He looked much smaller than expected. When she tried to reach her hand out to him, it was stopped by shackles attached to a far wall. "We'll have none of that, young lady. We all remember what happened last time."

A hidden crowd laughed in unison. Startled she tried to sit up but her head hit the ceiling. That's when she realized she was either really large or everyone else shrunk.

A Game

#379

"You must excuse us," said the tiny King upon his throne, "you're the first to actually drink from the Rabbits' flask. Up until now we weren't sure what would happen."

The girl used her elbows to sit up as much as possible while chained to the ground. She could hear faint murmurings around her. The voices of scared people watching her every move. "I would like to be set free and sent back to my home. I don't want to be here anymore."

The crowd laughed out loud, again. "I'm afraid that isn't possible. Whosoever drinks must win or die."

Red Girl

#380

Everyone sat and stared at the girl. Waiting. And waiting. And waiting…

"Will someone please tell me what is happening?" she cried out.

The King was about to speak when there came three knocks on the chamber door. He nodded for two guards to open the door. In walked a young woman, not unlike the giant. But she was battered and bruised. Her eyes searched the room, mad with fright.

She walked around the giant girl, staring at her. Was she looking in a mirror? Then she laughed. She laughed so loud and so long, she started turning bright red!

Redder Than Red

#381

When Red stopped laughing, the others tried to disappear into the shadows. They knew what they had done to her and hoped she had forgotten. She pointed a bony finger at the giant girl and spoke a language no one understood.

Peeking through a nearby window the sun started to rise, glowing blood red. Redder than Red. When the rays touched the giant girl's skin she felt herself begin to shrink. The room was finally the right size and her shackles no longer restrained her.

The King fled under their noses. But sitting on his throne was the Red girl.

Time

#382

Red grunted and I understood her every word. She is me from years ago. The first time I jumped off the platform. The first time I discovered this world by accident. The majority of her time, my time?, spent here was lived in the maze. A place full of mystery. A place occupied by others of me.

"We should find them," I said, hoping she would agree with my suggestion. But she wasted no time in letting me know it was a bad idea.

In the maze lived a queen who knew of my arrival and her hobby? Collecting hearts.

The Storm

#383

Not willing to sit idly by while a woman was out there stealing hearts, I decided to go, with or without Red. She relented. As I knew I would.

The deeper into the maze we got, the more frightened I became. We held each other's hand and stayed close. We mustn't ever touch the maze, she grunted. There were creatures that hid within the twine and twigs and branches, just waiting for their next meal.

Suddenly, the sky grew dark much too soon. The sun had only just risen. We looked up just as large raindrops fell from the sky.

Blue Girl

#384

The rain fell so violently, we were knee deep in raging waters. It had no place else to go but up and we were powerless against it.

There was something about the way it engulfed us that made me trust the water and I let it lead me wherever it wanted me to go. I wish I could say the same for Red. She tried to fight and struggled unnecessarily the entire time.

When the water started to lower we found ourselves face to face with another one of us. Only she wasn't red, she was most definitely dark blue.

No Escape

#385

There was something about Blue. Maybe it was her tear streaked face, pleading for us to save her. Or the way she held her hand out for me to take it. And I did. Trusting her felt much easier than I ever felt with Red. But we brought her along anyway.

Blue said no words. Her face told me everything I needed to know. With fewer words (or grunts) she managed to convey a sense of hope that I had lost long ago. We ran through the winding maze even though we knew escape was hopeless. We're all mad here.

Speak Rose

#386

Blue touched a nearby hedge and a blue colored rose bloomed. She then plucked it and handed it to me. A kind gesture? Or so I thought…

"She wants to know what took you so long to find her!" I wasn't expecting the rose to shout at me and nearly dropped it from the shock. It had no face but its delicate petals seemed to move when it spoke.

"How long has she been here waiting?" I asked, afraid of the answer.

"184 days exactly. But who's counting…" I've never encountered a sarcastic flower before. "So, did you bring it?"

The Brooch

#387

I didn't exactly now what the "it" was that I was supposed to bring. Then Blue began to cry and I immediately searched my pants pocket. Maybe I had something and just forgot all about it.

I felt something prick my finger. "Ouch," I said, sucking my pointer finger that had a spot of blood on it. I could see it was a brooch, but Blue snatched it from my fingers before I could get a better look.

"Is that it? The thing I was supposed to bring?"

The smile on Blue's face told me all I needed to know.

No Reflection

#388

Blue pricked her finger intentionally and handed the brooch to Red who did the same. We each held our fingers up and touched them together. If I had known ahead of time what was going to happen I don't know if I would've done it.

The pain that coursed through me was so severe all I could do was let out a blood curdling scream. When I opened my eyes I was alone. Where was no Red. There was no Blue. There was only me. Even the maze was gone.

In a room with a mirror, I had no reflection.

The Clock

#389

She tapped the mirror just to be sure it was real. And her reflection was really missing. She pursed her lips and crossed her arms. It just didn't make any sense.

She pondered for such a long while why her reflection was noticeably absent that a frog in a three piece suit bumped her, assuming she was nothing more than another garden statue.

Suddenly, a church clock began to strike a bell for each hour. How long had she been standing there? When the clock stopped she noticed right away, a face in the mirror. But it definitely wasn't hers.

Trapped

#390

With a sly grin, the face in the mirror winked. Then vanished. Her face was replaced by another. This one again was far different than the last but her sly grin resembled that of fear and anxiety. Her eyes were large and wide. Her lower lip trembled. She could not seem to walk away from the mirror, though she desperately wanted to.

When her face vanished, leaving behind the true reflection, it was then when she realized who those girls were. They were her. Having traveled to this place long ago. And like her they were trapped with no escape.

Home

#391

She walked up to the mirror and, letting curiosity take over, she reached out her hand towards the glass. As she expected, her hand went straight though it. But before she could pull it back out again she felt a hand grab hold of hers tightly. It pulled her through with much force until her entire body had stepped into the mirror.

"Dear? Dear?" A voice standing over her snapped their fingers in front of her face. "Have you been listening to me at all? I swear you're getting more and more absent-minded."

She recognized the familiar voice of home.

ReMemories

#392

"Mom? Is that really you?" Her shaky voice unsure as she stared at the woman in the middle of the kitchen. It was the most vivid memory she had of her mother and it felt so real.

"Of course it's really me," her mother answered. "Is it really you, I often ask myself. The daughter who never pays attention because she's too busy daydreaming. I used to daydream like you. Till I saw myself in the mirror, that is…"

She closed her eyes and listened to her mother talk. Trying desperately to hold on to the sound of her voice.

Five Dragon Riders

#393

The five dragon riders take to the sky in search of another child abducted by the nightstalkers. Winged beasts who cannot fly but use claws on their hands and feet to climb and run at impressive speeds. The nightstalkers only come out when the sun goes down as it burns their skin. And their eyes, sensitive to the moon's light, are a milky white.

Taking children while parents are asleep is not uncommon but the dragon riders are ready for the hunt. Their leader points to the peak of a mountain. Eyes aglow signals a possible end to their search.

The Morning Meal

#394

Hidden behind a row of thick trees was an entrance to a cave near the top of the mountain. Home to many nightstalkers and their food supply. The hunters had returned with a child, bound, gagged, and perfect for the morning meal.

They placed the child on the ground near a fire to keep warm during the night and also to keep a watchful eye. They could hear the familiar sound of dragon wings in the distance and knew the dragon riders must be circling just outside.

The riders found a clearing to land and unsheathed their swords for battle.

Tamryne

#395

A young man with long auburn hair pulled back in a ponytail that fell to his waist, held his sword against his chest as he gave orders to the others.

"Remember why we are here. When you spot the child, signal the others. I won't lose another tonight." Tamryne, the leader's older sister, took the lead into the cave. Everyone crouched low and listened for the familiar sound a nightstalker made. Their hands and feet skittering along the walls and ceiling.

Tamryne placed a finger over her lips and moved her eyes to the ceiling where a nightstalker was watching.

Bryndale

#396

The nightstalker dropped from the ceiling, its outstretched arms lunged for Tamryne. Without hesitation she raised her sword and pierced it clear through the beasts abdomen. She lowered it to the ground and pulled her sword, covered in crimson and black blood, free.

Her fellow dragon riders gave her a pat on the back. Silent congratulations for her first kill. They knew it would not be her last as the sound of scurrying could be heard echoing throughout the cavern.

Bryndale, her younger brother, raised his hand; five fingers. Five more beasts to deal with.

Then a child cried out.

Slain

#397

The dying embers of the ceremony left the four remaining dragon riders feeling somber. A fallen rider demands that their body receive a proper rest wherever they were slain.

Tamryne and Bryndale stood side by side, the glow of the fire in their eyes. "We must head back," Bryndale said, walking past the child who held Tamryne's hand tightly.

The remaining four dragon riders flew took to the sky. The fifth dragon flying solo. Leaving behind the slaughtered carcasses of the nightstalkers, slain in battle.

Tamryne glanced back towards the mountain's peak just as an arrow struck her dragon's wing.

Sacrifice

#398

Falling from the sky. One dragon retracted its injured wing and used the other to wrap Tamryne and the child. Protection from the impact they would make with the ground. A dragon is joined with a rider till the end and will always give its own life first without hesitation.

Then three dragon riders followed. They dove to try and catch them. But the weight of the riders slowed the speed of the dragons. All except the lone dragon, now riderless. It knew what must be done.

Without its rider there was just one solution, one sacrifice left to make.

Branches and Wings
#399

To an innocent bystander down below looking up, they saw five dragons descending towards the earth. One of them spiraling out of control. Then they are obscured by trees near the base of the mountain they just left.

Branches broke around them. Bryndale shouted orders to the others to save the child. He knew his sister could take care of herself. They practiced all their lives what to do in the event their dragon was shot down. But the child would be helpless.

The wounded dragon rolled to take the brunt of the impact before unfurling its one good wing.

Lone Dragon

#400

Tamryne and the child tumbled to the ground and lay unconscious. Surrounded by the other dragons and their riders, Bryndale pulled an amulet from around his neck. He held it up to the lone dragon. The rectangular shape of the prism created multicolored lights that bounced around the ground from the glow of the moon.

"Are you ready?" He asked the dragon. It bowed its head, ready to accept its fate. Bryndale smashed the crystal on the ground in front of the dragon. Light spilled out surrounding them all. The shriek was deafening. Then silence.

The lone dragon was gone.

"There is no greater agony than
bearing an untold story inside you."

— Maya Angelou

to be continued...

themes index

Themes are how I come up with the ideas for the stories you've just read. I hope knowing this information will help you better understand why I wrote each one and you'll go back to reread and see how they are uniquely connected.

Story #301 - #305

Creatures of the Night (Halloween Tarot) | Pages 10 - 19

Creatures of shadow and light and everything in between provide guidance and foresight through their distinct emotions and personalities.

Story #306 - #322

It Starts With You | Pages 20 - 53

Fellow fiction writers contributed the first sentence (no more than ten words) for each of these stories. I owe them a debt of gratitude for helping me out.

Mystic Madness (Suit of Wands) | Pages 54 - 81

Two heroine journeys reimagined through tarot. Get ready to experience tarot in an epic new light!

Ace of Wands - Glinda's Wand - Spotlight, pg 54

Two of Wands - Enchanted Forest - Two Paths, pg 56

Three of Wands - Chess Valley - Company, pg 58

Four of Wands - Munchkin Country - Wen and Fen, pg 60

Five of Wands - Croquet with the Queen - Rat Game, pg 62

Six of Wands - Dorothy's Triumph - A Win & A Lie, pg 64

Seven of Wands - Alice's Defense - Red River, pg 66

Eight of Wands - The Looking Glass Railway - Mosquito, pg 68

Nine of Wands - The White Knight - In Case of Emergency, pg 70

Ten of Wands - Bill the Lizard - Break Free, pg 72

Page of Wands - Scraps the Patchwork Girl - Don't Trust the Chicken, pg 74

Knight of Wands - Jack Pumpkinhead - Pumpkin Head, pg 76

Queen of Wands - Billina the Hen - The Caged Bird, pg 78

King of Wands - Prince Inga - The Kid, pg 80

Story #337 - #366

National Poetry Month | Pages 82 - 141

Each year the month of April is set aside as National Poetry Month, a time to celebrate poets and their craft. For this month I wrote 30 poems in 30 days that are each exactly 100 words in length. It was not easy but a challenge I was more than happy to undertake.

Launched by the Academy of American Poets in April 1996, National Poetry Month is a special occasion that celebrates poets' integral role in our culture and that poetry matters. Over the years, it has become the largest literary celebration in the world, with tens of millions of readers, students, K–12 teachers, librarians, booksellers, literary events curators, publishers, families, and—of course—poets, marking poetry's important place in our lives.

Story #367 - #392

Mystic Madness (Major Arcana) | Pages 142 - 193

Get ready to experience tarot in an epic new light!

0 Fool - Alice - The Jump

I The Magician - The Mad Hatter - The Watcher

II The High Priestess - The White Queen - It

III The Empress - Ozma of Oz - An Old Friend

IV The Emperor - The Wizard of Oz - The Run Away

V The Heirophant - The Blue Caterpillar - Butterfly

VI The Lovers - Dorothy and Scarecrow - The Maze

VII The Chariot - The Flying Monkeys - Multiplicity

VIII Strength - The Cowardly Lion - Meal

IX The Hermit - The Dormouse - Drunk

X Wheel of Fortune - The White Rabbit - Sober!

XI Justice - The King of Hearts - Big Head

XII The Hanged Man - The Tin Woodman - A Game

XIII Death - Teh Wicked Witch of the West - Red Girl

XIV Temperance - Aunt Em - Redder than Red

XV The Devil - The Queen of Hearts - Time

Story #393 - #400

A collection of 8 stories that, when read together, create a much larger story about a dragon. And who doesn't love a story about a dragon?

The Fifth 100

With each set of one hundred 100 word stories that I write, I feel like my skill level and ability can only get better. These books are my way to keep record of my efforts. The good, the bad, the ugly. Not all of my stories are masterpieces. I fully admit that.

But stick with me! There are some real bangers that you'll enjoy and even some that you'll never forget. As always, it's my nature to shock and terrify the only way I know how: horror.

In this collection I try to lean 100% to my love of horror.

acknowledgements

In two years I've had an entire community behind me, encouraging me and motivating me in so many ways, to keep going with my crazy 100 word stories journey. This book is a result of that journey that will continue for as long as they are with me.

Some of the people from that amazing community of fellow fiction writers and supporters of my storytelling work are:

Bill H.
Kim H.
Diana
Ben M.
Gloria
Edward
Liza D.
Natalie P.

about me

Erica L. Drayton was born in the Bronx, in NYC. She began writing stories almost immediately after she learned how to read and write from her mother, a former English teacher. As a gay, black, woman, Erica used storytelling as a way to express her feelings through poetry and fantasy novels at a young age.

After college, she took her continued passion for storytelling and developed it further, into writing short stories, eventually challenging herself to write 100 word stories.

She lives with her wife, young son, two dogs, and eight chickens in the Capital Region of Upstate New York.

erica drayton writes

Erica Drayton Writes is a newsletter that sends daily 100 Word Stories as well as updates on her countless other writing projects. She doesn't just write 100 word stories every single day. If that weren't enough, she also does all she can to inspire others to write 100 word stories on a regular basis.

If you subscribe today, you will receive a story every day that will make you think and one day give you the bug to try your own storytelling.

You can also upgrade for access to her comprehensive archive of 100 word stories, serials, and much more.

www.ingramcontent.com/pod-product-compliance
Lightning Source LLC
Chambersburg PA
CBHW042103160726
48295CB00017B/969